# Doll's Talk

*Also by Jean Richardson*

Four Little Swans and a Prince
Ballet Stories to Read Aloud

## *Other Collins Red Storybooks*

# Doll's Talk

JEAN RICHARDSON
ILLUSTRATED BY KATE ALDOUS

CollinsChildren'sBooks
*An imprint of HarperCollinsPublishers*

First published as *The Doll Fight*
in Great Britain by Hamish Hamilton Ltd in 1996
Published by CollinsChildrensBooks in 1998
1 3 5 7 9 10 8 6 4 2

CollinsChildrensBooks is an imprint of
HarperCollins*Publishers* Ltd,
77-85 Fulham Palace Road,
Hammersmith, London W6 8JB.

Text copyright © Jean Richardson 1996
Illustrations copyright © Kate Aldous 1996

ISBN 0 00 675205 5

The author and illustrator assert their moral right to be
identified as the author and illustrator of this work.

Printed and bound in Great Britain by
Caledonian International Book Manufacturing Ltd,
Glasgow, G64

# 1. The Birthday Present

SHELLEY WAS THE perfect doll.

The moment she lay down she shut her big blue eyes, and she had golden curls that could be washed and combed. Her best dress, which was the same shade of blue as her eyes, was trimmed with lace, and with it she wore long white socks and matching blue shoes. Shelley had lots of other outfits too, and she could drink, blow bubbles, and roller skate. Best of all, when you pressed her tummy, a tiny voice said, "I love my mama" and "Mama, tell me a story."

The only problem with Shelley was
that she belonged to Jenny's best
friend Sue, and she was far nicer than
any of Jenny's dolls.

Jenny wanted a doll like Shelley
almost as much as she wanted a
bicycle.

It was her birthday soon. She
guessed that Mum was buying her a
bicycle, but what about Gran? Gran
always asked what Jenny wanted.

Jenny told Mum how much she wanted a doll like Shelley so often that she was sure Gran would get the message.

As Gran lived miles away, her present came by post. This year the parcel was long and thin and hard. It didn't feel at all like a doll, but Jenny thought that perhaps the doll was in a long, thin, hard box.

It wasn't the first present she opened. Mum had given her a bicycle, and of course Jenny wanted to try it out at once. So it was some time before she looked at Gran's present.

Gran had wrapped it up very well. It took Jenny several minutes to undo the string and tear off all the wrapping paper. The card inside said: "*To dear Jenny, wishing you a very happy birthday. I hope Dora will say as much to you as she did to me. Lots of love, Gran.*"

Jenny tore off yet more paper and

came to what looked like an old shoe box. She jerked up the lid, and then stared. Inside was indeed a doll, but it was not like any doll she had ever seen.

For one thing, the doll looked much older than Jenny. Her hair was piled up in a sort of nest on top of her head. Delicate brows arched above her closed eyes. She had plump pink cheeks, a small rosebud mouth that just parted to show several pearly teeth, and a dimple in her chin. She was wearing a dark blue dress that was so long it came down to her ankles. The dress looked as though it was years old and needed a good wash.

"Good heavens!" Mum said. "Gran's sent you Dora. I used to play with her. Fancy Gran keeping her all these years."

Jenny was so disappointed that she

couldn't even be bothered to take
Dora out of the box.

"I don't want an old doll like this,"
she said. "I want one like Shelley, with
hair you can wash and lots of pretty
clothes."

And at the thought of Shelley's
washable curls and her wardrobe of
party frocks, Jenny burst into tears.

"Gran didn't mean to upset you,"
Mum said. "I'm sure she thought
you'd like Dora."

"But you knew the kind of doll I wanted," Jenny sobbed. "Why didn't you tell her?"

"Dolls like Shelley are quite expensive," Mum said. "I didn't think Gran could afford one. That's why I didn't tell her you wanted a doll. She must have guessed."

"But she didn't want to spend any money," said Jenny rudely. "She sent me some old thing that didn't cost anything. Well, I hate Gran, and I don't want her horrid doll."

And with that she picked up Dora's box, marched upstairs and shoved it under her bed. "I don't ever want to see you again," she said. "I was having a really super birthday until you turned up."

Mum didn't say any more about Gran or Dora. She was too busy getting everything ready for Jenny's party.

Jenny tried to forget Dora, though it was hard to forget her when Sue arrived with Shelley. Shelley was wearing her blue party frock, and Sue had brushed out her curls and put on her blue velvet headband. Jenny could cheerfully have jumped on Shelley.

The party went on for hours. They played Pass the Parcel, Hide and Seek and Grandmother's Footsteps. Sue's

dad, who'd come to help, barbecued
burgers and sausages, and then
everyone sang "Happy Birthday" as
Jenny cut her cake.

When it was time to go home,
everyone was given a book, a balloon
and some sweets. Sue said Shelley
wanted a present too, so Mum found
her an extra balloon.

Although it was long past her
bedtime, Jenny was too excited to
sleep. She lay in bed going over
everything that had happened on her
birthday.

She couldn't help feeling cross with
Gran, because Gran had let her
down. She and Jenny had always been
special friends, which is why she'd
known Jenny wanted a doll without
being told. She could at least have
sent me some money, Jenny thought.
Even her Auntie Jane, who was so

high-powered that she never had time
to leave her office to go shopping, had
sent a gift token.

If I added my savings to the token,
Jenny thought, perhaps I could buy
the kind of doll I really want.

She was trying to decide whether
the doll should have fair or dark hair
and she was almost asleep, when a
sound nearby startled her.

Someone sneezed.

Jenny was wide awake at once.
Atishoo! There it was again. A small
but definite sneeze, and it seemed to
be coming from under her bed.

Jenny felt for the torch she kept
under her pillow. She pushed back her
duvet, bent over the side of the bed
and shone the torch.

The beam of light picked out her
slippers, her teddy, who was always

falling out of bed, her beach ball, which was too big to fit into the toy cupboard, and the box that contained Dora. She was puzzled. Neither her slippers, nor her teddy, nor her beach ball had ever sneezed.

Atishoo! Atishoo! Atishoo! This time it was several little sneezes. They seemed to be coming from Dora's box.

Jenny dragged out the box and pulled off the lid. The doll opened her eyes, sneezed again, and said in a tiny cross voice: "What sort of a welcome is this?"

"You sneezed." Jenny couldn't believe her ears.

"What do you expect! I've probably got a chill. I got very cold on my journey. I was looking forward to a little warming soup and a comfortable bed. Instead, someone lost her temper and pushed me somewhere dark and

dusty. It's enough to make anyone sneeze."

"You can talk!" Jenny thought she must be dreaming.

"Of course I can talk," said the doll. "I'm not a baby."

"But dolls don't talk. Well, some do, but they can only say a few words like 'Mama'."

"Nonsense! All the dolls I know can talk."

"But . . ." Jenny was lost for words.

"Mind you, I'm not surprised yours don't talk if you treat them like this. I shan't say another word until you're nicer to me." The doll shut her eyes and closed her rosebud mouth very firmly.

She's right, Jenny thought. I haven't treated her very well. She got out of bed, picked up the box and very gently took Dora out of it. Then she carried her over to the chair where her other dolls were sitting with a little quilt tucked round them. She pulled back the quilt and put Dora in the middle of the dolls, where she hoped she would be comfortable and warm.

"I'm sorry I haven't any soup," she said, "but I'll get you something nice tomorrow. I promise."

The doll's eyes remained shut and she didn't reply.

When she was back in bed, Jenny wondered whether she'd imagined the whole thing. But just before she fell asleep, she was sure she heard another very small sneeze.

## 2. Dolls' Clothes

JENNY THOUGHT ABOUT Dora as soon as she woke up.

She jumped out of bed and ran over to the chair where she had put her. She'd left Dora sitting in the middle of the dolls, but now she was lying on her back with the quilt pulled up to her neck. None of the other dolls had moved.

Jenny picked up Dora. Her eyes didn't open, not even when Jenny began tipping her backwards and forwards.

"Do you want me to be sick," asked a small voice, "because I shall be, if you go on doing that?"

Jenny stopped at once and stared down at the doll. So it wasn't a dream after all. She really did talk.

"I'm sorry. I was trying to make you open your eyes."

"I open them when I want to," snapped the doll. "Do you need to be shaken to open your eyes?"

"No, of course not." Jenny tried to think of something polite to say. "Did you sleep well?"

"As well as anyone can when they're still in their travelling clothes and not in a proper bed. Don't you get undressed when you go to bed?"

"Yes, but you don't have any other clothes to put on. I mean," Jenny saw that the doll was looking even crosser, "you didn't bring any other clothes with you."

"The postal service is a disgrace. I

was told that they would be delivered
first post."

"Perhaps they'll come this morning,"
Jenny said, hoping to soothe the doll.
"I'll come and tell you after
breakfast."

Dora didn't look very pleased, and
Jenny was glad when Mum shouted
that breakfast was ready.

As it was the holidays, Jenny didn't
have to get ready for school. But as

Mum had to go to the office, Jenny
was going to spend the day with Sue.

Jenny wondered what Sue would
think of Dora. She didn't have lots
of smart clothes like Shelley, but
then Shelley couldn't talk, well, not
properly.

She went upstairs to fetch Dora. She
was beginning to feel proud of her.
Although the faded blue dress made
the doll look old-fashioned, Jenny saw
now that she had
a very pretty face.

Mum, who was always late for the office, said, "Sorry, I can't stop," as soon as Sue's mum opened the door. She didn't even notice Shelley, who was wearing a polo-neck shirt, tight fawn trousers, boots and a black helmet.

"Look what Auntie Jo sent," Sue said to Jenny.

"Shelley's dressed to go riding, and she's got lots of other new clothes. Perhaps some of them'll fit your dolls."

Jenny did sometimes wish that Auntie Jane would send her presents like this, but not today. Today her thoughts were full of Dora.

"Guess what?" she said. "I've got a new doll. Well, Dora's an old doll really, but she can talk."

"Dora!" Sue said. "Why's she called Dora?"

"Because it's her name. It's what Gran called her."

"What a silly name," said Sue. "I've never heard of anyone called Dora, but I know lots of people called Shelley."

Jenny was too excited to argue. They went upstairs to Sue's bedroom, where there were dolls' clothes all over the floor.

"Ugh!" said Sue, looking at Dora for the first time. "What a funny doll. Why's she wearing that awful dress? Did your Gran send that too?"

"She's not funny," said Jenny. "And her dress is just old, that's all." She'd noticed that Dora was looking furious.

"Let's hear her talk, then," said Sue, and before Jenny could stop her, she pressed Dora's tummy.

Nothing happened.

"You said she could talk," said Sue, jabbing her finger into Dora several times.

"You don't have to do that," said Jenny, snatching Dora away. "You just talk to her, and she answers back."

"I'm sorry," she said to Dora, "Sue didn't mean to hurt you."

Dora's eyes were shut, but Jenny saw that her cheeks had turned pale.

"I don't think Dora's feeling very well," she said.

"Perhaps her battery's run out," said Sue.

"She hasn't got a battery. She doesn't need one. She's . . ." Jenny was about to say alive, but she wasn't sure that Dora was.

"Why don't we give her something nice to wear," said Sue, who was longing to play with her dolls' clothes.

"Some of these would probably fit her. She's about the same size as Shelley."

Jenny wasn't sure that Dora would like to wear Shelley's clothes, but it seemed better than trying to make her talk. She laid the doll on the bed and began to undo the tiny buttons of her dress. When she pulled the long skirt over Dora's head, she and Sue stared in surprise.

Neither of them had ever seen underwear like Dora's. Her vest had long sleeves, her knickers were more like breeches and came down to her knees, and she was wearing rose pink stockings.

Sue wanted to take everything off, but Jenny felt a shudder go through Dora's body.

"Let's put Shelley's clothes on top,"

she said, hastily pushing Dora's arm
into a flowered shirt.

"That shirt goes with these mauve
dungarees," said Sue, stuffing Dora's
legs into them.

The flowered shirt and the mauve
dungarees were a good fit, but somehow
Jenny felt they didn't look quite right
on Dora.

Even Sue noticed that the doll didn't
look pleased. "What a grumpy face
she's got. She hasn't got a nice smile
like Shelley."

Just then, Sue's mum called up to say it was time to go shopping.

"Let's leave the dolls," said Sue, sitting Shelley on her bed. Jenny put Dora beside her. She hoped the two dolls would get on together and that perhaps Dora would teach Shelley some more words. It would be fun if both dolls could talk – though she didn't want Shelley to be as clever as Dora.

They were so long at the shops that when they got back it was time for lunch. Then Sue wanted Jenny to try her new swing, and after that they played in the Wendy house. There was so much to do that they forgot about the dolls, and Jenny only remembered Dora when Mum arrived to collect her.

They found the two dolls sitting side by side on the bed where they'd left

them. Shelley was still dressed to go
riding, but Dora was wearing her old
dark blue dress. The flowered shirt
and the mauve dungarees were folded
up neatly beside her.

Sue was so busy undressing Shelley
that she didn't notice what had
happened.

"Look," Jenny said, "she's changed.
Dora was wearing Shelley's clothes
when we went out."

"I suppose my mum changed her," said Sue.

"Why would she? How would she know which was Dora's dress?"

"Well, someone did. Dora couldn't have changed herself."

"But she did," Jenny insisted. "She must have."

"First you say she can talk. Now you say she can change her clothes. But she can't. You just want to pretend that she's cleverer than Shelley."

Sue ran downstairs and Jenny heard her telling her mother that silly old Jenny was pretending her doll could talk.

"But you can," Jenny said to Dora. "And you did change your clothes, didn't you?"

There was no answer. Dora's eyes were shut, and Jenny couldn't bring herself to try and shake them open.

Perhaps Sue was right, and she had imagined it all.

She took Dora downstairs, thanked Sue's mum for looking after her, and walked down the road with Mum. She had so wanted to impress Sue, but it hadn't worked out like that. Dora had let her down, and Jenny was tempted to dump her in someone's front garden and tell her to find her own way home if she was so clever.

She looked down at Dora. Her eyes were still firmly shut, but as though she could read Jenny's thoughts, the doll said three words very clearly: "Don't you dare."

# 3. Dolls on Skates

DORA'S EYES WERE still shut the next
morning. Jenny felt so annoyed that
she gave the doll a good shake.
Nothing happened. Dora wouldn't
open her eyes.

"You're a silly, stupid, obstinate,
naughty, lazy doll," Jenny said.
"I thought you were special, but
Sue's right, you're not."

She put Dora back among the other
dolls and didn't bother to tuck the
quilt round her.

During breakfast the postman
brought a parcel for Jenny. She saw

Gran's writing on the label. It said:

*To Miss Dora, c/o Jenny Johnson*

She was about to open the parcel
when Mum said, "But it isn't
addressed to you. I think you should
wait until you've finished eating, and
then take the parcel to Dora."

Jenny thought Mum was being silly,
but she gave in.

Back in her bedroom, she took the
parcel over to Dora and said, "It's for
you."

The doll's eyes opened at once. "I
expect it's my clothes," she said.
"Please unpack them."

It was another shoe box – what a lot
of shoes Gran must buy, Jenny
thought. Inside, neatly folded, were
not only dresses but more long
knickers, a nightdress, three hats, one

with a splendid feather and a jewelled hatpin, a suit, a handbag, and a small square of brown velvet on a tiny cord.

Jenny was trying to decide what this was when Dora said, "I'm so glad they've sent my muff. My hands do get very cold."

"You changed your clothes yourself yesterday, didn't you?" Jenny said.

"Of course. You didn't expect me to stay in those awful trousers, did you?

And if you must undress me, please
don't do it in front of other people.
No lady ever takes off her clothes in
public."

"Well, may I take them off now?"
Jenny asked. "I want to see what you
look like in these."

" I should like to wear my tweed
suit," said Dora.

Jenny took off Dora's dark blue
dress and folded it carefully before
putting on her tweed suit. The suit
was trimmed with brown velvet. It had
a pleated skirt with a tasselled cord
round the waist, and a jacket with tiny
gilt buttons. The outfit included a
brown velvet beret.

"Have you a looking-glass?" Dora
demanded when Jenny had finished
dressing her.

Jenny held Dora up in front of the
mirror and the doll adjusted her hat.

"I like the bow to one side," she said, "and I need my hatpin and my muff."

Jenny found the tiny pin, which was very sharp, and Dora stuck it firmly in her hat. Then she tucked her hands inside her muff.

"I'm ready for my walk," she said. "Shall we go?"

This time when they arrived at Sue's, Shelley was wearing a bright pink anorak, a very short skirt and mauve tights. On her feet were a pair of pink and mauve roller skates.

Jenny saw Dora looked shocked.

"Look," she said to Sue, "Dora's clothes have arrived. Doesn't she look smart."

"She looks like a little old lady," Sue said. "Let's go outside and I'll show you how Shelley can roller-skate."

They went out into the back garden

and set up house under the apple tree.
Sue's dad had just mowed the lawn, so
the grass was very short and smooth.

Sue stood Shelley on the grass and
pressed a button in her back. Shelley
rolled forward a few steps and then
fell over. Sue picked her up and started
her off again. Shelley fell over again.

"She's not very good," said Jenny,
secretly a little pleased.

"She was very good yesterday," said

Sue. "It must be the grass. It's too lumpy. I'll try her on the path."

Shelley did a little better on the path, but then stopped.

Sue pressed her button a few times, but Shelley didn't move. "Her battery must have run out," Sue said. "She won't do anything without a new one."

"Dora doesn't need a battery," Jenny said.

"But Dora can't skate."

"I bet she could – if she had some skates."

"Well, she can borrow Shelley's. Go on, let's see what silly old Dora can do."

Jenny wished she hadn't spoken. Sue was already pulling off Shelley's skates and shoving Dora's feet into them.

"I can't get her boots off," she said. "But her feet are so small it doesn't matter."

"You're hurting her."

"Don't be silly." Sue held Dora above her head as Jenny made a grab at her.

"Give her back. She's mine!" Jenny leapt at Sue and they rolled over on the grass as Sue let go of Dora.

"I'll break Shelley into little pieces if you hurt Dora," Jenny yelled.

"Don't you dare," Sue said – and then her voice changed. "Look!" she whispered.

Jenny looked.

Dora had got to her feet and taken off. She was skating down the path. Not in the stiff way that Shelley had done, but by lifting each foot and propelling herself forward.

As Jenny and Sue watched, Dora reached the end of the path, made a neat turn and began skating back to

them. Her muff was slung over one
shoulder. She spread out her arms as
though she was about to take off and
zoomed forward on one skate, the
other leg in the air.

She had almost reached them when
the cat pounced. It had been sitting
on the fence, its eyes on stalks. It had
never seen a bird like this.

Knocked off balance, Dora fell sideways and lay on the grass, face down. The cat sniffed her, decided she wasn't something to eat, and backed away. Jenny ran to pick up Dora. She put her on her feet, but the doll couldn't stand.

"Her battery must have run out too," Sue said, "or else the cat's broken her."

"She hasn't got a battery," Jenny said, worried that perhaps Dora was hurt. "I'm going to take her inside to lie down."

She carried Dora upstairs and laid her gently on Sue's bed. She put a pillow under her head, and tucked the duvet round her.

"You're all right, aren't you?" she asked anxiously.

"A little bruised," Dora said faintly. "Nothing some arnica won't cure."

"I don't think we've got any of that," Jenny said. "Mum puts antiseptic cream on me when I fall over."

"Don't bother. It was my own fault. I'm really too old to skate, but I couldn't resist showing your friend that I'm not 'a little old lady'."

"You were wonderful. How did you learn?"

"I was Dolls' Roller-Skating Champion for 1921, 1922, and 1923," Dora said. "Then I took up bicycling instead."

"You were miles better than Shelley."

"Ah, poor Shelley," Dora said. "Thinks she knows it all. Couldn't be more wrong."

And with that she smiled, closed her eyes and fell asleep.

# 4. Looking Pretty

IT TOOK DORA several days to get over her fall. Jenny looked at her every day, but the doll kept her eyes closed. Jenny decided that this was Dora's way of saying that she wanted to be left alone.

On Friday Jenny and Sue had planned to take the dolls for a ride round the garden in Sue's dolls' pram, but the sun went in and it began to rain.

"What are we going to do?" wailed Sue, looking round at all her toys as though she had nothing to play with.

Jenny would have been happy playing with Sue's doll's house, or her post office, or her toy cooker, which had mini-saucepans and a dinky frying pan.

"I know what we'll play," said Sue. "Let's give the dolls a beauty treatment. There are lots of things on Mum's dressing table we can use."

"Won't she mind?" Jenny was sure her mother wouldn't like it.

"She won't know," Sue said. "Laura from next door has popped round for coffee, and they never notice anything when they're talking."

They crept into Sue's mum's bedroom and, sure enough, the dressing table was littered with all kinds of make-up. Sue grabbed a handful of bottles and jars and so did Jenny. They took them back to Sue's bedroom.

"Let's give the dolls a manicure,"
said Sue, who'd seen her mum doing
her hands. "First we rub cream into
their hands and then we can paint
their nails."

There was every shade of varnish,
from the palest pink to brilliant red.
Sue chose Flamingo Pink, Jenny,
Dragon Fire. She wondered if Dora
would complain about being given
scarlet nails, but when she looked at
Dora's hands, she could see traces of
red paint.

Painting such tiny nails wasn't easy.
Brushes made for grownup hands
dripped great blobs of colour. Soon
both dolls had pink and red hands,
and the carpet had matching spots.

"I'll get some remover," said Sue.
Luckily the varnish came off easily,
though not off the carpet.

Sue suggested they should practise
on their own nails first, so she painted
Jenny's Flamingo Pink and Jenny
painted Sue's Dragon Fire. Afterwards

there was just the right amount of varnish left on each brush for the dolls' nails. Soon everyone had smart hands, though Jenny thought that Dragon Fire looked nicer on Dora than on Sue.

Next Sue found some blusher and face powder, blue and green eyeshadow and several lipsticks.

Dora didn't need any blusher, but Jenny powdered her nose. Trying to put lipstick on her rosebud mouth wasn't easy. Much of it went on Dora's pearly teeth. Jenny hoped she wouldn't ask to look in a mirror.

Then Sue and Jenny put some make-up on themselves. Sue brushed blue all round her eyes and made her lashes stand out like spikes. When Jenny laughed at her, Sue scribbled on Jenny's face with lipstick. Jenny gave Sue a red nose, and by the time they'd finished they looked like a couple of clowns.

Then they sprinkled themselves and the dolls with perfume. Although it looked like a big bottle, there wasn't much in it and it was soon empty.

"Now let's wash the dolls' hair," Sue said. "Then we can set it and spray it with lacquer."

"You can't wash Dora's hair," Jenny said. "I don't think you're even supposed to comb it."

"That's why it looks like a bird's nest," said Sue. "Shelley's hair is lovely to wash. Let's go in the bathroom and I'll show you."

What a pity I can't wash Dora's hair, Jenny thought, as Sue tucked a towel round Shelley, dipped her fair curls into the water and started rubbing them with shampoo.

"Can you get me a comb and

Shelley's hairbrush," said Sue as she rinsed Shelley's hair and began drying it with a towel. "They're on the chest of drawers in my bedroom."

As soon as Jenny had gone, Sue seized Dora.

"Now it's your turn," she said. "Your hair needs a good wash. Jenny's just being silly leaving it so dirty."

She began to pull at Dora's bun. It

seemed to have been stuck on with
glue, because although Sue tugged at
it she couldn't undo it. She was afraid
that any minute Jenny would come
back and stop her.

"I'll just have to wash it as it is," she
said, but as she went to duck Dora's
head in the water, she felt a sharp
pain in her hand. It was as though
she'd been jabbed with a needle, and

when she looked down, she saw a long thread of blood.

Sue screamed.

Jenny and Sue's mother came running.

"That doll attacked me!" Sue said. "Look at my hand. It's all bleeding."

And indeed several large drops of blood had appeared on her hand.

"You must have scratched it," said Sue's mother, rummaging in the bathroom cabinet for a plaster.

"I didn't," sobbed Sue. "That doll did it. She stuck something in me."

Suddenly Sue's mother noticed Sue's scarlet nails and her clown make-up.

"What have you two been up to?" she said. "That's my new lipstick! That's my best nail varnish!"

She rushed out of the bathroom and Sue and Jenny heard her wailing, "There's powder and varnish all over the carpet! And my French perfume! Do you know what that perfume cost!"

By the time everything had been found and put back, and the worst spots had been cleaned off the carpet, Dora's attack on Sue was forgotten.

It was when she was putting Dora to bed, that Jenny found the hatpin stuck in the folds of Dora's dress.

"What's this doing here?" she asked. "I nearly scratched my hand too."

"I always take it with me for protection," Dora said. "And just as well. Heavens knows what would have happened if that silly little girl had washed my hair."

"You mean you scratched Sue on purpose?"

"I had no choice. She was about to ruin my hair. My hair was styled by Monsieur Alphonse, the finest hairdresser in Paris, and NO ONE is allowed to touch it."

Just then, Jenny's mum came in. "What's all this about you sticking a pin in Sue? Sue's mum has just told me Sue has a very nasty scratch on her hand."

"It wasn't me, Mum, it was Dora," Jenny explained. "She didn't want Sue to wash her hair."

"Don't be silly, darling," Mum said.

"I know you like to pretend that Dora does things, but it's not a game when it comes to sticking pins in people. It could be dangerous."

"But I didn't," Jenny insisted. "I've told you, it was Dora. Why don't you ask her?"

"Well don't let Dora do it again," said Mum firmly. "Dora's your doll, and you're responsible for her, just as I'm responsible for you. Is that clear?"

Before Jenny could say any more, Mum pounced on the hatpin. "Wherever did that come from? It looks lethal. I don't want you playing with anything like that."

Jenny held her breath as Mum stuck the hatpin firmly in her lapel. For a moment, she'd wondered if Dora would dare to attack Mum.

"She's grown up quite well, all things considered," Dora said, after

Mum had left the room. "I had a lot of trouble with her, I can tell you."

And she did tell Jenny.

When she was in bed, Dora sat on her pillow and told her how naughty Mum and Auntie Jane had been when they were little.

It was the best bedtime story Jenny had ever heard, and Dora promised to tell her lots more – tomorrow.

## 5. Pinched

"WHY CAN'T SHELLEY talk?" Jenny asked Dora. "You said all dolls can talk."

"They can," said Dora, "but not if they've been brainwashed. Shelley's only been taught to say a few words, so that's all she can say."

"Who taught you?" Jenny wanted to know.

"All my mothers," said Dora. "When I was made, dolls were expected to stand on their own feet. There was none of this spoonfeeding them with 'I love my mama'. It's such nonsense.

Supposing you don't love your
mama?"

"But all dolls love their mothers,"
said Jenny. The idea that any of her
dolls might not love her was an
uncomfortable one.

"Love isn't a duty," Dora said. "Love
has to be earned. You don't really
think that all the dolls who are thrown
about, or left out in the rain, or shut
up in dark cupboards love their
mothers."

"But you love me, don't you?" asked Jenny, waiting for Dora to say she did.

Dora took her time. "Sometimes, more often than not," she said at last. "As long as you behave properly."

"And if I don't?"

"Then I certainly won't love you. And you can't make me." Dora's mouth snapped shut in a way that made it clear there was to be no argument.

Mum called up to say that it was

time to go to Sue's. There wasn't time
to change Dora's dress, but Jenny
wiped her face gently with a tissue
and made sure that her hair was as
Monsieur Alphonse would have liked
to see it.

Sue had a doll's house and every
time they played with it, Sue seemed
to have something new for the house.
Today it was things for the kitchen: a
tiny fridge, an ironing board with a
minute iron, a cooker, and a dresser
with shelves of little blue and white
plates.

Sue and Jenny took all the furniture
out of the house and then pretended
that they had just bought it and were
moving in. It was Jenny's turn to
furnish the bedroom, and she wanted
the little rocking-chair as well as the
double bed and the chest of drawers
and wardrobe.

"That goes downstairs," said Sue, snatching the rocking-chair.

"But it's upstairs today," said Jenny, grabbing it back.

"No it's not. There aren't any chairs in the bedroom."

Sue always got her own way. "It's my doll's house, it's my Wendy house, it's my slide, it's my swing . . ." Everything was always Sue's.

Sometimes Jenny felt that Sue had everything she wanted.

Jenny felt so cross about the rocking-chair that when Sue wasn't looking, she stuffed it into her pocket. Serve her right, she thought.

When Jenny got home, she took out the rocking-chair and put it on her chest of drawers. It looked small and lost away from the doll's house, and somehow she didn't want to play with it. She hid it in her chest of drawers, under a pile of knickers, and part of her wished that she hadn't bothered to take it.

Jenny was so looking forward to hearing more about Mum and Auntie Jane that she couldn't wait to go to bed. As soon as Mum had kissed her goodnight, she put Dora on her pillow, and waited for the story to begin.

Nothing happened.

"Tell me about Mum and Auntie Jane," she said. "You promised to tell me more."

Dora didn't answer, and Jenny saw that her eyes were shut.

"What's the matter?" she asked.

"Put it back," said Dora. It was an order.

"Put what back?" Jenny pretended not to know.

"The rocking-chair you stole."

So Dora had seen her.

"I'm ashamed of you," Dora went on. "Taking something that doesn't belong to you. Whatever next."

"Sue's got masses of things. She's always having presents. She won't even miss it."

"Some people have more things, and some people have less," said Dora. "That's no excuse. You must never take what doesn't belong to you. You're a thief."

It was an ugly word. It made Jenny feel mean and ugly. And angry with Dora.

"Why don't you mind your own business," she said.

"You are my business," snapped Dora. "I kept an eye on your gran and her mother before her, and on your mum and your Auntie Jane. All of them were a credit to me. They may have been naughty sometimes, but they didn't do wrong."

"What are you going to do about it then?" Jenny asked. "Tell the police. Tell Mum. They won't believe you. No one believes you can talk except me, so there."

"I'm not going to tell anyone," said Dora, "not even your gran, who most certainly would believe me. I'm not going to say another word. You can get yourself another doll to talk to. Why not steal one like Shelley, if that's how you want to behave."

She meant it. Dora's face was as closed as a shop with its shutters down. It was as though she had gone away.

Jenny picked up Dora and threw her across the room. The doll landed with a thud. Jenny felt scared. Perhaps she

was broken. She pulled the duvet over her head, but she couldn't shut out her thoughts.

Dora was special. Jenny hadn't felt lonely for a moment since she'd arrived. Dora was more fun than any other doll because she had a mind of her own. Jenny wanted Dora to love her, to admire her, to think she was great. Dora knew all about her.

Jenny pushed back the duvet and got out of bed. She went over to the bundle on the floor, picked it up very gently and carried Dora back to bed.

"I'm sorry," she whispered. "I didn't mean to hurt you. And I will take the rocking-chair back. I don't want to be a thief."

The shutters were still down. Perhaps Dora had banged her head and was unconscious.

Jenny cradled Dora in her arms and willed her to get better. "I'm really, truly sorry. I'll never hurt you again. I promise."

"I should hope not." The voice was very faint, but it was unmistakably Dora's.

## 6. The Museum of Toys

ONE DAY NOT long after the end of the holidays, when Jenny and Sue were back at school, their teacher Mrs Puddicombe told the class that they were going to visit a very special museum.

"It's a collection of toys," she explained. "There are dolls, teddies, doll's houses, toy soldiers, books and games. Many of them are very old, so we'll be able to see the kind of toys your mums and dads, your grandparents and even great-grandparents played with. Mrs Dean, who looks after the museum, thought it would be nice if you all took a favourite toy to show her the sort of toys you like."

Everyone looked forward to having a day out. Mrs Puddicombe had pointed out that the toys must be small and easy to take on the bus. So when the class lined up, they were carrying dolls and teddies, puppets, stuffed animals, and model aeroplanes and cars.

Jenny of course had brought Dora, who was wearing her best suit and brown velvet hat.

"I must look my best," Dora had insisted. "There's no knowing who I might meet. I have a cousin who went to live in a museum."

Shelley was also looking her best. Several of the class had dolls like her, but no one had a doll like Dora.

"Jenny says her doll can talk," said Sue, "but I've never heard her. My

doll really can talk," and she squeezed
Shelley who obediently said "I love
my mama".

"Make your doll say something,"
said Nicholas, who was carrying an
enormous teddy bear called Rupert.

"Dora only talks to me," Jenny said.
She saw that Nicholas didn't believe
her.

When the class got off the bus, Mrs
Puddicombe counted everyone to
make sure no one was left behind, but
she hadn't time to count the toys as
well. "Hold on tight to them," she
said. "We don't want any lost dolls."

When they got to the museum, Mrs
Dean was waiting for them. She led
them past the showcases to a room
with tables and chairs and lots of
space.

They began by looking at some tops.
Some of them were very old, but they

were still brightly coloured, and when Mrs Dean spun them, they whirled round in dazzling patterns.

Then Mrs Dean showed them some of the museum's treasures. There was a Noah's ark that opened to reveal the Noah family and all the animals. The ark was more than a hundred years old, so everyone had to be very gentle with the small wooden animals. There were jumping jacks who could still leap up and down, little tin toys that had cost only a penny, a horse and cart from the days before cars, and a clockwork figure who played the violin. There were also toy railway-engines and toy cars, and a bear who was nearly ninety years old and had lost much of his stuffing. Last of all, came the dolls.

Many of them, Mrs Dean said, would have been sold undressed and

their clothes made by dressmakers or
the owner's mother. Some were
dressed like ladies of fashion, others
looked more like children.

As they crowded round Mrs Dean
and her assistant to take a closer look,

Jenny found herself staring at a doll who could have been Dora's sister.

She was about to show the doll to Dora, in case it was her cousin, when the assistant in charge of the dolls began to collect them up. She held out her hand for Dora.

"No, she's mine," said Jenny, hugging Dora to her.

The girl didn't believe her. She tried gently but firmly to remove Dora.

Jenny hung on to Dora tightly. "Leave Dora alone," she said. "She's mine. I brought her with me."

The girl went away and came back with Mrs Dean, who said at once, "No, that's not one of ours. But may I have a look at her?"

Jenny wasn't sure. She didn't want Dora to be snatched away and imprisoned in a glass case.

"I'll take great care of her," Mrs

Dean promised. "I can see she's a very special doll. Why don't we go and look at her in my office."

Jenny felt very important as she and Dora followed Mrs Dean to her office.

"Now," said Mrs Dean, when she and Jenny had sat down and Dora was lying on the desk in front of them, "tell me about her. Where did she come from?"

While Mrs Dean was examining Dora very carefully, Jenny told her about Gran, and how Dora had arrived in a shoe box.

"And do you play with her?" Mrs Dean asked. She seemed to be looking for something, and her face lit up at the sight of a number on the back of Dora's neck. Jenny had never noticed it.

"Yes," Jenny said, "but Dora isn't

just like any other doll. "She's very special."

"She's probably even more special than you realize," Mrs Dean said, getting up and fetching a book from her shelves. "There aren't very many dolls like Dora left. Most of them got broken and thrown away. Dora has obviously been very well looked after."

"She's mine." Jenny picked up Dora quickly, in case Mrs Dean wanted to keep her.

"I know, but in some ways a doll like Dora is almost too special to play with." Mrs Dean was looking through the book as she spoke, and now she pushed it across the desk to Jenny. Jenny found herself looking at a photograph of Dora. "For one thing, she's worth a great deal of money."

"How much?"

"I can't say exactly. But dolls as rare

as Dora can fetch thousands of pounds
at auction. We might even be interested
in buying her for the museum."

Thousands of pounds! Jenny couldn't
take it in.

"I need to do some research to find
out just how rare Dora is," Mrs Dean
went on, "so I wonder if you would
consider leaving her with me, just for
a few days. I'd take the greatest care

of her, but I'd like to show her to
some of my colleagues. When you
come to fetch her, I'll be able to give
you and your parents a better idea of
how much she might be worth."

Jenny didn't know what to say. She
didn't like the idea of parting with
Dora, even for a few days, but it was
very tempting to think that she might
be worth a fortune.

"I'll give you a receipt for her,"

Mrs Dean said, "and I promise it will only be for a few days."

Jenny would like to have asked Dora, but she didn't think that Dora would say anything in front of Mrs Dean.

"All right," she said. "But only for a very few days."

Mrs Dean wrote Jenny a note on the museum's headed paper. She showed it to Jenny before putting it in an envelope. "Give me a ring next week,"

she said, "and we'll arrange a time for you to collect Dora."

Jenny folded up the envelope and put it in her pocket where she knew it would be safe. Mrs Dean sat Dora on a shelf, where she too would be quite safe.

Then they went back to join the class, who were busy exploring the museum.

There was lots to see, but all Jenny could think about was that Dora was worth thousands of pounds. She wanted to go home straightaway and tell Mum.

But when Mum came to collect Jenny from Sue's, she had important news of her own.

"A colleague at the office is ill, and I've got to fly to New York tonight in her place. I'll only be away a few days, and Gran's coming to look after you."

"But Mum –" said Jenny.

"It's a wonderful chance for me," Mum went on. "I couldn't say no. It could mean promotion and more money for us. We might even get a new car."

Jenny saw that Mum was already miles away in New York. It was no use trying to tell her about Dora. All she could think about was catching her plane.

"I'll have to tell Gran," Jenny thought. And then she saw that Gran, who had given her Dora, was just the right person to tell.

## 7. *True Value*

IT WAS FUN having Gran to stay. She
was supposed to be looking after
Jenny, but it was really the other way
round. Jenny helped Gran get supper.
They had it on trays in front of the
TV because Gran didn't want to miss
her favourite soap. Afterwards, when
Gran was washing up and Jenny drying,
Jenny told her about Dora.

"Did you know she was worth a lot
of money when you gave her to me?"
she asked.

"No, I didn't," said Gran. "I
remembered that I'd liked playing

79

with her when I was your age, so I thought you would too."

"But you knew she was special. You told me on the card, though I didn't understand what you meant. You said you hoped Dora would say as much to me."

"And does she?" asked Gran, who was busy wiping down the cooker.

"Yes, but why doesn't she talk to Mum? Mum didn't believe me when I told her."

"I'm sure Dora used to talk to her," said Gran, who was determined to make the cooker shine like new. "But your mum's forgotten. People tend to forget things like that when they grow up and lead busy lives. Dora doesn't talk to me any more, but I hoped she would to you."

"Why doesn't she talk to you?"

"I suppose I'm too old," said Gran

sadly. "There are some things you can only do when you're six or seven. One day you'll be too old for Dora, and then she won't talk to you any more. But if you have a daughter, Dora might talk to her."

"She won't be able to if I've sold her," Jenny pointed out. "Gran, would you mind if I did?"

"I'd be a little sorry," Gran said, stepping back to admire the gleaming cooker, "but it's up to you. Dora is your doll now."

Later on, lying in bed, Jenny thought of all the things she'd be able to buy if she sold Dora for thousands of pounds. All the toys Sue had. A doll's house. A slide. A swing. She saw herself asking Sue round to play and this time she'd be the one who had everything.

Everything except a doll who could really talk.

Jenny had been so busy thinking of all the things the money could buy that she hadn't thought about not having Dora.

If the museum bought Dora, Mrs Dean would put her in a glass case, so that no one could touch her or play with her. She wondered what it would feel like, and whether Dora would mind.

Perhaps the toys come out at night to play, she thought. Perhaps Dora would enjoy having dolls of her own age to talk to. Jenny wasn't sure, and the more she thought about it, the harder it was to fall asleep.

She remembered all the fun she'd had with Dora. How Dora loved being read to, and liked the same stories as Jenny. How she would watch Jenny paint a picture – and then tell her how good it was.

Jenny was too grown up to be frightened of the dark, but it felt lonely without Dora. Gran had read her a bedtime story, but even she had other things to do. Dora never had to get meals ready, or do the dusting or the ironing. She was there whenever Jenny needed her.

That night Jenny dreamed that Dora
was lost and she was looking for her
everywhere. When she woke up, the
feeling of loss was like a pain inside
her. The relief when she realised that
it was only a bad dream, was like a
shout of joy. Dora wasn't lost after all.

Jenny knew then that she couldn't
sell Dora, even for thousands of
pounds.

"I don't want to sell Dora," she told
Gran over breakfast. "I don't want a
doll like Shelley that can only say 'I
love my mama'. Not after having
Dora."

"You don't have to sell her if you
don't want to, dear," said Gran.
"Nobody's going to make you. Just tell
the museum lady what you've decided.
It's up to you."

"Will she be cross?"

"Of course not. I'll ring and tell her
that we'd like to come and collect
Dora because we both love her far too
much to part with her."

When they got to the museum, they
were shown into Mrs Dean's office.
Dora was sitting on Mrs Dean's
desk and Jenny snatched her up and
cradled her in her arms. She felt as

though she hadn't seen her for days.

Mrs Dean smiled. "I gather you don't want to part with Dora," she said, "but I'd like to ask you a favour. Will you bring Dora in one day and let us take her photograph, so that we have a proper record of her? She's a valuable doll so you must take great care of her. Perhaps when you're older and don't want to play with her any more, you might lend Dora to us."

"Would I be able to have her back?"

"Of course. She'll increase in value as she gets older, and one day you might want to sell her. Or you might like us to look after her."

Jenny couldn't imagine a time when she wouldn't want to talk to Dora, but as Gran had warned her, one day Dora might stop talking to her. That would be the time.

Jenny didn't say much on the way home, but she held Dora very tightly. Accidents could happen.

"You made a wise decision, if I may say so," said Dora later, when she and Jenny were tucked up in bed. "I never thought I should want to retire, but after a few more years of looking after you, I think I'll be ready for a glass case. I'm glad I shall be with dolls of my own age."

"What do you mean, looking after me?" Jenny said. "I'm the one who does the looking after."

"Are you?" said Dora. "Well, in that case, perhaps you wouldn't mind undressing me. I don't like sleeping in a dress. It gets so creased."

She shut her eyes and Jenny knew she wouldn't say another word until she got her own way.

So she got up, undressed Dora and put on her frilly nightdress.

Dora opened her eyes and smiled. "That's better. Now what about a nice game of I Spy? I spy with my little eye, something beginning with M."

But Jenny had to wait until next morning to find out what Dora had spied. After all the excitement of the last few days, she was so tired that she was soon fast asleep.

# SPIDER McDREW

## by Alan Durant

Spider McDrew is a hopeless case. Everybody says so. He's so busy dreaming he's often one step behind everyone else. But he does have a special talent for surprises. Whether playing football or performing in the school play, Spider *always* has a surprise in store.

# DIMANCHE DILLER
by Henrietta Branford

When Dimanche is orphaned at the tender age of one, Chief Inspector Barry Bullpit advertises for any known relative to come forward. Unluckily for Dimanche, her real aunt does not see the message – but a bogus one does! So Dimanche, who is heir to an enormous fortune, is sent to live with the dreaded Valburga Vilemile, who tries to rid herself of Dimanche at every opportunity. Her lack of success owes itself to Polly Pugh, who looks after Dimanche, foils all attempts to polish her off, and helps her find her true aunt.

In 1995, *Dimanche Diller* won the Smarties 7-9 category Fiction Award, a prize awarded for the year's most exciting piece of children's fiction.

£2.99

# Order Form

To order direct from the publishers, just make a list of the titles you want and fill in the form below:

Name .................................................................................

Address ...........................................................................

.........................................................................................

.........................................................................................

Send to: Dept 6, HarperCollins Publishers Ltd, Westerhill Road, Bishopbriggs, Glasgow G64 2QT.

Please enclose a cheque or postal order to the value of the cover price, plus:

UK & BFPO: Add £1.00 for the first book, and 25p per copy for each additional book ordered.

Overseas and Eire: Add £2.95 service charge. Books will be sent by surface mail but quotes for airmail despatch will be given on request.

A 24-hour telephone ordering service is available to holders of Visa, MasterCard, Amex or Switch cards on 0141- 772 2281.

Collins
An *Imprint* of HarperCollins*Publishers*